Abducted

Lauren Mitchell

ISBN: 1986242714

ISBN-13: 978-198624

CHAPTER ONE

"Go, Zach!" Jamie exclaimed.

"You can do it!" yelled Nicolas.

Zach gave a nervous smile as he stepped up to the bat. The whole team was counting on him to make the winning hit. He picked up the bat and tilted his head up, spreading his feet apart. The crowd stared intently as they waited for the ball to be thrown. As the ball barreled through the air, the crowd sat quietly, anticipating the moment he would hit the ball. Zach swung, and looking as surprised as the crowd, watched as the ball sailed out of the park, and into the woods. The crowd went wild.

"Yeah Zack!" roared Jamie, "I knew you could do it!"

Zach walked proudly into the dugout, where his teammates praised and congratulated him. Jamie and Nicolas watched as their friend came out of the dugout, and headed towards them.

"Dude that was awesome!" Jamie said excitedly.

Zach smiled bashfully, his dark bangs covering his eyes. "Yeah, I guess it was pretty awesome. Coach is for sure putting me in next time."

They talked about Zach's game all the way home. They

stopped in front of Jamie's house.

"Well, I'll see you guys tomorrow." Jamie said.

"Bye!" Zach and Nicolas yelled in unison.

Jamie turned and walked up the sidewalk, noticing his parents' cars weren't there. Jamie sighed. He slid the key out from under the mat and unlocked the door. On his way to his room, he passed a photo of him and his parents. He glanced sadly at the photo. They were all smiling happily, their dusty brown hair and green eyes making them look more alike than ever. Ever since they had moved to Connecticut three years ago, he had hardly seen them. His dad was a surgeon at their local hospital, and his mom was the manager of the Cancer Research Center. They left at six o'clock in the morning and didn't arrive home until ten o'clock at night, sometimes later. His only time with them was some on Saturday, and Sunday if he was lucky.

Jamie entered his robot filled room, where posters of his favorite creations hung from deep blue walls. They were his inspiration when he created his own robots. His previous inventions stood on display all around his room. His favorite creation, Tommy, sat on his desk, where he was testing out new features to see how the robot would react to certain hand movement. He was using Tommy because he was his favorite out of all the other ones. He made him when he was ten, right after they had moved. They had had a special bond ever since. He crossed the room towards his desk, and began to work, taking notes on what he would respond to. So far he had down: Clap and thumbs up. Jamie nodded, proud of his progress he had made on Tommy on understanding human movements.

Looking over at the clock, Jamie realized he had been up for three hours working on his latest discovery.

"Well, that's all I can do tonight. Goodnight Tommy." Jamie climbed into bed and sighed.

If only you were here, Jamie thought sadly.

The next morning, Jamie got dressed and went outside to wait for Zach. They usually walked to school together.

"Hey Jamie," Zach greeted when he saw him, "remember we have that test today in science."

"Oh crap! I completely forgot!" Jamie exclaimed.

"It's okay, you can borrow my notes." said Zach encouragingly.

"Thanks." Jamie said with a smile.

"At this time, all workbooks and study guides need to be put away." stated Mr. Brown plainly.

"I can't believe he's making us take this test after one week," whispered Freddie, Jamie's best friend.

"I thought you knew everything," Jamie whispered back.

"Well everything but science, I'm failing in here! My last

report card was a 96!"

Jamie rolled his eyes. "Just because you don't make all one hundreds doesn't mean you failed."

"Jamie be quiet! There are tests out and I don't take it that you want a zero." scolded Mr. Brown sharply.

"Sorry, Mr. Brown." Jamie said annoyedly.

"Hey, do you guys want to go explore the forest?" asked Nicholas as they left the school. "Sure," Jamie said shrugging, "can Leslie come?" Leslie was one of the boys' best friends. "Doesn't she have after school detention?" asked Freddie.

"Oh yeah I forgot, I guess we'll see her tomorrow." Jamie answered.

The boys crossed the road and jogged into the entrance of the forest, a place that they loved to explore and sometimes hang out in. A cool wind seeped through the trees of the dark woods as evening fell.

"This place is kind of creepy at night," Freddie said nervously, moving closer to the middle of the group.

"First of all it isn't night time, and second of all, we come here all the time, there's nothing scary here." Jamie scoffed.

Nicholas rolled his eyes, "Guys, let's just head back and we can come back tomorrow with Leslie."

They turn around and start to leave. Zach stayed back.

"Hey guys, I think I'm going to stay here for a while. You know, look at the stars and have some time alone."

"Whatever you say," Jamie said, "see you tomorrow."

Jamie, Nicholas, and Freddie headed back home. Zach laid on a patch of grass, gazing up at the stars. He liked to have alone time. Time away from everybody, time to think. Suddenly he heard a noise. He sat up and looked around. "Who's there?" he asked, swallowing the lump in his throat. He stood up and looked at his surroundings. Hearing nothing, he decided it was just the wind. As he laid back down, he froze. There he saw it. The big, monstrous shadow slowly coming towards him, its bright yellow eyes burning him. It was slowly creeping towards him, like a lion stalking its prey. It grew closer and closer until he could feel its cool breath gently blowing against his face. Zach looked up in terror, seeing the creatures small, beady eyes looking down on him. Zach let out a shrill scream, as he watched the creature surround him.

CHAPTER TWO

"Hey, where's Zach?" questioned Nicholas.

"I don't know, he didn't walk to school with me this morning and he won't answer the phone," Jamie said, looking nervous.

"We can go over to his house to check on him," Freddie suggested, "I don't have anything to study for."

Jamie nodded. "Yeah, I guess. Leslie should be out anytime."

They headed over to the side of the school and sat down on the grass.

"Hey guys," Leslie said, walking over and sitting down next to them, her blonde hair glowing in the sunlight. "what's up?"

"We were going to go over to Zach's to make sure everything is okay. He didn't show up at school today," informed Jamie.

"He's probably just sick, the flu has been going around like crazy." Leslie said encouragingly. "Yeah, you're probably right." answered Jamie.

Just as they started to leave, the school bullies, Jack

Davis and Henry Ellis walked up. They had been mean to Jamie and his friends since the beginning of school. "Well, well, well. If it isn't the losers again. Where are you punks heading?" Jack snarled at Jamie and crossed his arms. Henry stood next to Jack, his bulging muscles sticking out from his broad frame.

"Uh, we were just going-"

"Home," Leslie quickly explained, cutting Jamie off. "we were going home."

Jack smirked, taking a step closer to Leslie. She gulped and looked up at Jack, who towered over her.

"You think you're tough, huh? Jack scoffed. "A girl like you, who can't even manage to talk to the teacher? A girl who just sits there like she's dumb?" Jack smiled at Henry and the boys looked satisfied with themselves. Leslie's face turned bright red and she looked down at the ground. Nicholas glared at Jack. He lowered his head and started breathing heavily.

"Oh no." muttered Jamie. Freddie looked nervously from Nicholas to Jack.

"No one messes with my friends!" exclaimed Nicholas, heading towards Jack.

"Nicholas-" started Leslie.

"I'm tired of people like you trying to hurt other people because you aren't happy with your own sad life!" Nicholas lunged at Jack, who hardly budged.

Jack chuckled. "You're messing with the wrong person, dork." Jack leaned forward and pushed Nicholas into a mud pile, splashing a big glob of mud all over his face. Nicholas gasped. Jack and Henry walked away, whispering and laughing at each other.

"Nicholas, are you alright?" asked Leslie compassionately.

Nicholas sighed. "Yeah, I'm fine. I can't believe he gets away with that." Nicholas glared towards Jack, who was now walking over to a different group of kids.

"It's fine, let's just go over to Zach's and make sure everything's okay." Jamie said.

As they approached Zach's house, they noticed something was wrong. Police cars flooded the front of Zach's house. Officers were searching around the house, and some were asking questions to Zach's mom, clearly looking worried.

"I knew something was wrong." Jamie said, looking around frantically. The friends ran up to the front porch, searching for someone to talk to. Mr. Jones, Zach's step-dad, stared anxiously out the window.

"What's going on?" Freddie asked hesitantly.

"I don't know," Leslie answered, sounding shocked. "but it can't be good."

"Mr. Jones," Jamie started. "what's going on?"

"Zach was with you all last night. He never came home. Have you guys seen him?" Mr. Jones looked hopefully at the boys.

"N-no, we haven't." stuttered Jamie.

"He was with us in the woods last night. It started getting dark so we wanted to go home. Zach told us that he wanted to stay back in the woods. We haven't seen him since." explained Nicholas. Mr. Jones put his face in his hands and took a deep breath.

"I'm really sorry," Jamie said quietly.

Leslie turned her face to look out the window. Tears fell softly down her face.

"C'mon let's go." Jamie headed for the door.

Once they had managed to get out onto the street, they stopped abruptly at the end of the road. "What are we going to do?" asked Freddie, looking at Jamie gloomily.

Jamie glanced out at his surroundings. "We're going to find Zach. He's out there somewhere. He's my best friend, we can't just sit around and do nothing. It's been almost a whole day." Jamie turned to the group, looking intently at each one of them.

"I'll go," answered Nicholas bravely.

"And me." Leslie said, still looking slightly down.

"Uh… I guess I'll go," Freddie answered unsurely. "For Zach."

"For Zach!" repeated the others in unison.

"Okay, first let's explore the woods. That's where we saw him last." Jamie turned left, heading towards the towering trees, swaying slightly in the wind. An eerie feeling sweep over them as they entered the dreadful place, where their friend had mysteriously disappeared.

"It's cold in here." complained Freddie, lifting his arms over his chest. They continued going along the path that was all too familiar, searching in vain for their friend.

Night came, and all that could be heard was the rustling of the leaves and owls who perched up in trees, looking down on the friends with yellow eyes that glowed in the darkness.

"I think we should head back." Nicholas said disappointedly.

"You're right," Jamie said. "we can come back tomorrow. We can't give up."

They turned around, cautious of their steps. As they exited the brush, Jamie hesitated, looking at the forest.

"You coming?" asked Nicholas.

Jamie turned around and followed his friends back towards the road. As Jamie unlocked the door to his house, he wondered if something more had happened to Zach. Something more than just getting lost, and he knew it wasn't good whatever it was.

<u>CHAPTER 3</u>

Jamie woke up to the sound of something in the kitchen. He sat up alertly, listening closer. He heard it again. It sounded like something going through the cabinets, shuffling around the kitchen. He slowly climbed out of bed and tiptoed to his door. He opened it slowly, peeking around the corner, careful not to make any noise. He shuffled down the hallway, then down the stairs, stepping carefully into the living room. The light was on in the kitchen. Jamie's heart started to pound. As he slowly approached the kitchen, he heard voices.

"I can't believe this happened. He must feel so awful!" whispered one of the voices.

"Yeah," said the second voice. "Jamie doesn't deserve this."

At the sound of his name, Jamie burst into the kitchen. He stopped abruptly when he saw his parents standing at the counter drinking coffee. "Wh-what are you doing here?" he stammered, shocked to see his parents there. They turned around at the sound of Jamie's voice. His mom smiled.

"We decided to take a day off so we could stay home with you, " her smile quickly disappeared. "Where was he the last time you saw him?" she asked, a troubled look crossing over her face. Jamie frowned. "We went to the forest together and when we were going to go home he said he wanted to stay there for a while by himself. I guess he never came back."

"Ah I see." his mom said with a sad smile.

"I'm sure they'll find him soon," his dad said reassuringly. "you don't have to go to school today if you don't want to."

Jamie nodded. "Thanks."

Jamie headed back up the steps towards his room. He sat on the edge of his bed, thinking about everything that had happened. It makes no sense, Jamie thought to himself. Why did Zack just disappear? He walked over to his window, where he saw Nicholas standing on the porch. He ran down the steps and opened the door. "What are you doing here?" Jamie asked, looking confused.

 "Leslie and I have been talking and we've decided that maybe Zach ran away because something was bothering him," Nicholas said slowly.

"What do you mean?" Jamie asked curiously. "Like what?"

Nicholas looked up at Jamie, a worried look in his eyes. "Well," Nicholas started slowly. "me and Leslie got together and decided to hack into some files. We searched up Zach's dad, and it turns out he's been charged. It didn't say what for. He was imprisoned for six months before being bailed out by one of his brothers. After doing more research, we found that he had moved to Ohio because he had been kicked out by Zach's mom and had nowhere to stay. He recently moved back here to Connecticut, but we haven't figured out why." Nicholas paused.

Jamie stared at him. "So you're saying what exactly?" he asked, looking overwhelmed by everything Nicholas was saying.

"I've seen this car pull up to Zach's house almost every day, and I think it's his dad, He ran away because his dad is," Nicholas stopped. "hurting him." He finally said.

Jamie frowned. "But there's no proof," he replied angrily. "Zach wouldn't just run off like that. I know him better than that! He wouldn't do that!" Jamie yelled.

"Jamie, why do you think he's been so down acting lately? Besides, he told us he wanted to stay behind in the woods. That's not like him, he never wants to go in there even with us in the daytime, let alone by himself at night. Think about it, Jamie-"

"No!" roared Jamie. "That's not what happened! He was never abused! He wouldn't do that! He's out there somewhere and it's up to us to find him!" Jamie stormed inside and slammed the door.

"Everything okay, sweetie?" His mom questioned as Jamie stomped up the stairs.

"Leave me alone!" he yelled slamming the door to his room. Jamie walked over to his bed and buried his face in his pillow. He rolled over to face Tommy. Jamie had a strong connection to Tommy, but for some reason every time he looked at the robot a sad feeling swept over him.

He looked away, tears blurring his vision. He suddenly heard a knock on his door.

"Jamie," his mom called. "can I come in?"

Jamie didn't answer, instead, he rolled over to face the wall. The door opened, and the bottom of his bed sunk in as his mom sat down.

"Jamie, Nicholas told me what happened. Whether it was that or not, the police have been searching every area of the city. They're going to find him, no matter what happened."

His mom paused, waiting for Jamie to answer. Instead of answering, Jamie turned to look at a photo sitting in the middle of his dresser. Following his gaze, his mom found what he was staring at. Jamie turned to his mom.

"I've already lost him, I can't lose Zach too." Jamie's voice cracked as he remembered the dreadful day he would never forget.

His mom touched his arm. "Don't worry," she said as calmly as she could. "we'll find him soon. Until then, we have to stay positive and try to be happy." his mom smiled, then stood up and left the room, shutting the door behind her. Jamie walked to the bathroom and washed his face. Feeling refreshed he decided to go meet his friends to talk about what to do.

"Hey, Jamie!" Leslie greeted him.

"Glad you could make it," remarked Nicholas.

"I'm sorry about earlier," apologized Jamie. "I'm just really upset about everything that's going on."

"Don't worry about it." Nicholas said, avoiding Jamie's eyes.

"Hey guys I think I found something!" called Freddie from the woods in front of them. The friends walked over to where Freddie was standing, following his gaze towards the ground.

"It's Zach's figurines!" exclaimed Jamie. He bent over to pick them up. They gathered around to examine them.

"Zach wouldn't leave those behind for anything." commented Leslie.

"Exactly." answered Jamie.

"We have to take them to the police!" Freddie exclaimed.

"Jamie." called out a female officer, opening up a door to a room. She smiled at them as they stood up and approached her. The friends filed into the room and sat down in front of a large wooden desk with the name "WARDEN" engraved on the front.

"Officer Warden will be will you in just a second."

The woman smiled and closed the door to the small room. A few moments later, a tall, bulky police officer entered the room. He sat down behind the desk and looked up at the group.

"May I help you?" he asked, looking from one to another

of the friends. His gaze was intent, with his eyebrows furrowed.

"Well, we found something that may help with the case of Zach Peterson." Nicholas explained. "Ah, is that the missing kid?" Officer Warden asked.

"Yes," Jamie started. "we were in the woods and we found some of his action figures lying in a pile of dirt. He never goes anywhere without them." they all looked at the officer.

 "Ok," he muttered, jotting down notes in a notebook. "Do you have them with you?"

"Yes, they're right here."

Jamie handed them to the officer. He examined them carefully, setting each one aside in a plastic bag.

"We will examine these more and make sure to tell you all if we find anything. In the meantime, you kids need to stay out of trouble. Whoever took Zach is still out there." Officer Warden gave the kids a warning look.

"We will. Thanks, officer." Jamie stood up to leave.

"Call me John." he said to Jamie with a hint of a smile as him and his friends walked out the door.

"Thanks, John." Jamie repeated as he walked out into the cool autumn air.

"What do we do now?" asked Freddie.

"We look." Jamie started for the forest.

"For what?" questioned Freddie.

"More clues. Duh!" Jamie answered annoyedly. They walked down the trail and began to search for more clues that would help find their friend. Leslie stopped abruptly, a worried look crossing her face.

"Guys, did you hear that?" she asked in a panicked tone.

"Hear what?" Nicholas asked, stopping next to Leslie to listen. A hushed voice flowed through the air as if being carried through by the wind. It's him, the voice hissed. It's him! The voice got louder and louder. IT'S HIM! It screeched. IT'S HIM!

Leslie, Freddie, Nicholas, and Jamie ran as fast as they could towards the exit of the forest. Once they were far away, they stopped to catch their breath.

"What was that?" exclaimed Freddie in horror. They all shook their heads, confused about what had happened. Leslie looked pale.

"What did it mean by 'It's him'?" Nicholas asked.

"No idea," answered Jamie, still breathing heavily. "but I don't think that's normal."

"Do you think it could mean something bad happened to Zach?" Nicholas questioned.

"I don't know." Jamie stated, looking distraught.

"Since when do we believe random voices coming from

absolutely nothing in the woods?" Leslie asked annoyedly. "I mean, it may have been weird, but it can't have meant anything. I'm sure Zach's fine. Like Nicholas said, he probably is having family issues and he'll come back in a couple of days. Besides, the police are looking for him. He can't have gone that far." Leslie scoffed.

"It's already been a couple of days!" exclaimed Jamie heatedly. He's nowhere in sight, the police have searched every inch of the town! It had to have meant something. Call me crazy, but ever since Zach went missing I've had a bad feeling. Maybe he just ran away, but he's my friend. I have a bad feeling about this, and I'm going to find out what happened. You don't have to help me or come with me, but I think Zach would appreciate it if you did." Jamie looked around at his friends. They all stared back at him for a second, not sure what to say.

"I'm in." said Nicholas giving Jamie a nod.

"Me too," said Freddie. "Zach has always been there for us, I think it's time for us to return the favor." everyone turned to look at Leslie. She looked at the ground, avoiding eye contact with the boys.

"Les... " started Jamie. Leslie looked up at Jamie with a concerned look. Jamie watched her with pleading eyes.

"Ok." she answered finally.

The sun was setting as they walked back home, a beautiful color swept over the sky as the flaming ball slowly disappeared. Jamie walked up to his house, waving goodbye to his friends. As Jamie fell asleep that night, he wondered where Zach was and if he was ok.

<u>CHAPTER 4</u>

Jamie had finally convinced his parents to let him go to school. All of his friends were going to be there, so there was no point in him not going. He had been thinking about the voice in the woods. What had it meant? Jamie still had no clue. Maybe the voice was warning them about someone in their group. Or perhaps, it was trying to give him a clue to where Zach was, or maybe it was even trying to throw them off. He was almost certain Zach hadn't just run away, the voice clarified that. Jamie grabbed his usual breakfast; a granola bar with a glass of milk. Since this was his parents' last day off, he felt bad about leaving, but he needed to see his friends and talk about what had happened yesterday. As he stepped out onto the street, the red, orange and yellow leaves fell around him, making a beautiful swirl of color. It was slightly cooler than usual, although it was mid-October. As Jamie neared the school, a dreadful feeling washed over him. He knew the other kids would be talking about Zach, and Jamie didn't feel ready to talk about it. He took a deep breath and continued forward towards the school. As he walked up the steps, he overheard a group of kids whispering in the corner next to the railing of the steps.

"Did you hear about how that Pullman kid went missing?

"Yeah," replied another. "They say he just vanished."

Jamie quickly walked through the doors of the all too

familiar place. As he entered his first class, math, he looked around for Leslie, who was in his class. He didn't see her anywhere. He took his seat which was in the front row. He absolutely hated the front row because the teacher constantly called on him and he felt like everyone was staring at him. Jamie had just started on his pre-algebra worksheet when Leslie, looking exhausted and timid, entered the room. She shot Jamie the 'We need to talk' look as she passed Jamie to take her seat.

As Jamie entered the lunchroom, he scanned the room for Leslie. He found her sitting with a couple of her friends from a different class.

"Hey, Les." Jamie said casually, slowly walking up to her and her friends.

"I have to go," she told them, a little too enthusiastically. "bye!" she grabbed Jamie's arm and rushed him through the doors, the smell of pizza and cookies disappearing.

"Where are we going?" Jamie wondered out loud.

"Shhh!" Leslie hissed. She didn't let go of Jamie's arm until they had entered the library.

"Why are we here?" Jamie questioned, following Leslie to a nearby table. Instead of answering, she turned their chairs away from the doors. She sat down in one of the seats, obviously not knowing where to start.

"You were right." she started.

Jamie looked confused. "Ri- right... about what?" he stammered.

"Zach didn't run away, and he didn't disappear." she looked over at Jamie.

"Then what happened?" he whispered slowly.

"Jamie, last night while I was going to bed, I couldn't stop thinking about the voice." Leslie paused, then continued. "So I decided to take a walk. I walked down near the woods, and then I heard something." Leslie looked down at the desk as tears filled her eyes.

"What happened, Leslie?" demanded Jamie.

Leslie took a deep breath. "I heard a noise, it sounded like a man talking. It was coming from the forest, so I sneaked around to the edge of the ditch leading to the outer part of the forest. And there was a man there. He was walking with a kid." Leslie's voice cracked as she finished the last sentence.

"Was it-" started Jamie in horror.

"Yes, Jamie. It was Zach. I know it was! The voice, the way he walked, everything." Leslie stopped to let Jamie take in what was happening.

"So he was kidnapped!" exclaimed Jamie suddenly.

"Shhh!" barked Leslie.

But Jamie continued. "You saw it, he was walking with a man! You didn't think to tell someone like the police?" Jamie was now standing, looking down on Leslie.

"Jamie!" she exclaimed before he could continue. "He saw

me! The man saw me! He told me if I told anyone, bad things would happen to me and everyone I love." Tears poured down her face.

Jamie looked terrified, as he sat back down. "He saw you?" he asked Leslie gently.

She nodded. "I don't know who he was, I couldn't really see him. But he sounded weird, I've never heard his voice before. I couldn't see him either, but his eyes looked strange. They sort of glowed. I thought I would tell you today so he wouldn't know I told." Leslie stood up. "C'mon we have to go. Lunch is almost over."

As they walked back to class, Jamie couldn't help but think about what Leslie had told him. This is so weird, thought Jamie.

"Hey," Freddie said dully to Jamie, as they walked out of the school.

"Hey," Jamie replied. "what's wrong?" Freddie glanced over to Rosa, a girl in their science class. Her auburn hair appeared to be sparkling in the sunlight.

"You like her?" questioned Jamie with a chuckle.

Freddie turned bright red. "Don't laugh." he grumbled.

"Sorry," Jamie replied, still smiling. His smile quickly disappeared. "but there are more important things to worry about."

"Like what?" he questioned.

"Well, it requires going to the police station. But first, let's wait for Leslie and Nicholas to come out." he replied.

 Finally, Leslie and Nicholas walked out of the school and seemed to be talking casually.

"Hey." greeted Leslie, throwing Jamie a look. They formed a circle on the side of the schoolyard.

"So, Leslie said we had something to talk about?" Nicholas half stated half asked. Jamie gave Leslie a nod to indicate her to start the story.

"Ok," she started, waiting for the last bit of kids to leave the school. "I couldn't sleep last night, so I decided to take a walk. I walked down into the woods and I heard a noise. It sounded like a man talking. I got closer to see what it was, and there was a man wearing all black talking to a kid on the edge of the forest. The kid- the kid was, Zach. I could tell. It sounded like him and the way he walked- I know it was him. The guy saw me and told me bad things would happen if I told anyone. That's why I didn't tell the police. So I told Jamie today at lunch and now we are all going to tell the police so hopefully, they can find Zach." Leslie took a deep breath and looked around at the group, who all but Jamie stared at her dreadfully.

"So you're saying a guy took Zach and was walking around in the woods with him?" Freddie asked.

"That makes no sense!" exclaimed Nicholas. "Why would Zach just casually walk and talk in the woods with someone who kidnapped him?" Nicholas barked.

"I don't know," Leslie answered, shaking her head. "it doesn't make sense. I'm just telling you what I saw and heard." she looked pleadingly at the others.

"We're not saying we don't believe you," Nicholas answered as calmly as possible. "it's just that it makes no sense. Why would he do that?" Nicholas looked around as if searching for answers. "Well," Jamie chimed in. "we're going to tell the police, so they can find Zach and hopefully tell us what really happened." Jamie started towards the street. The others followed.

Once they had arrived at the station, they waited to talk to John. Freddie rocked back and forth nervously, looking intently at the wall in front of him. Suddenly John stepped out of his office. Seeing them, he smiled. They walked into his office and took the same seats as last time. "So what brings you here today?" he asked politely.

"Well, we have more news about Zach." Jamie told him.

John pulled out his notebook. "I figured so," he leaned back in his chair and crossed his arms, waiting for someone to speak. Everyone looked at Leslie. She shifted uncomfortably in her seat and cleared her throat, and began to speak.

Once she had finished, the group all looked up at the officer. He raised his eyebrows and nodded his head.

"That's interesting. But don't worry, we will get this taken care of. I just need to know some details about what you saw so I can send a search team and we can get your friend back." he smiled reassuringly.

"Thanks, John." Jamie said compassionately.

"It's just my job," John said smiling. "But on a different note, we've got some scans back from the lab about those action figures. The fingerprints show something, but we can't figure out what." John had a troubled look in his eyes.

"What do you mean?" questioned Nicholas.

"Well, the scanning shows a set of fingerprints, but it doesn't seem to match up to a human's," John answered slowly.

Jamie frowned. "What's that supposed to mean then?"

John shook his head. "I don't know. The whole thing is weird. But don't worry, the print most likely ran wrong, so we'll retest it. We'll get it all sorted out and find your friend." John gave a small smile to the group.

Jamie smiled back. "Thanks, John." he said again.

Later that day, Jamie was walking home from a game of basketball with his friends. After the good news at the station, he was in a particularly good mood. Maybe John and his team would find Zach after all. He didn't think much about the fingerprint, only because he knew the technology wasn't always right. As he rounded the corner onto the street, his stomach dropped. There at the corner of the road next to the Burger Place, stood the two people Jamie hated most. He quickly turned around and ran in the other direction. After making it home, Jamie panted out of breath up his driveway. He walked up to the door to unlock it, only to find it was already unlocked. He cautiously opened it. Peeking his head around the corner first, he entered. "Hello?" he called, slowly walking around the downstairs. He stopped. He heard voices coming from upstairs. More specifically, his room. He crept up the stairs, his heart pounding viciously. His parents' cars weren't in the driveway, so it couldn't have been them. He shuffled down the hallway, stopping just outside of his room. The door was cracked open slightly. Jamie remembered shutting it completely when he left that morning. Listening inside, he heard two voices.

"We fooled them!" the first called out in a deep raspy voice that chilled Jamie.

The second voice chuckled. A hideous, shrill shriek. "Yes!" he exclaimed. "Master will be very happy with us now. We gave him what he wanted."

"No," said the first again. "Master is not happy. We have to destroy them! We have to continue until every last one is destroyed!" both voices began cackling. The noise slowly faded away, only leaving behind their cold presence and Jamie who had heard everything they said.

CHAPTER 5

"Jamie, what's the matter? You aren't talking much." Nicholas stated as he shoved part of a cheeseburger in his mouth. They had just sat down for lunch.

"Something happened last night when I came home," Jamie replied.

"Yeah," Nicholas answered, swallowing a gigantic bite of food. "like what?"

"I don't know. The- these things were in my room. They were talking about how they fooled us. An- and how they had pleased their master and they needed to destroy the rest of us." Jamie stirred his mashed potatoes and shook his head.

"Sounds like a crazy dream to me," responded Nicholas, unfazed.

"But it seemed so real!" exclaimed Jamie. "The way they spoke. It was terrifying!"

"Maybe you need to get more rest," Freddie said matter of factly. "lack of sleep can lead to illusions and-"

"We get it," said Jamie rolling his eyes. "but this was real.

They really were there. I- I felt them. This awful feeling came over me and I felt kinda like I was dead."

"Alright, let's be real here," interrupted Nicholas. "Jamie, I think everything happening with Zach is getting to you." he declared.

Jamie sighed. "I guess. But what did it mean?" he asked.

"Nothing," replied Freddie and Nicholas at the same time.

"C'mon guys," said Leslie standing up with her tray. "it's time to go."

As Jamie worked on his robot later that evening, he thought about skipping school the next day so he could go down to the police station to check in with John about the case. Jamie knew what he had heard was impossible, but it didn't seem like a dream. The way they spoke made him feel empty like he didn't even exist. He went into the bathroom to brush his teeth because it was now eleven o'clock. He leaned over the sink, and in horror, leaned back. There in the sink were two blobs identical to slugs, emerging from the sink. The lights went out, and he saw things all over the wall. Things that weren't logic, or even in this world. Jamie screamed. He cowered in the corner, crying and screaming. His parents flung the door open and ran over to Jamie.

"Sweetie, what's the matter?" his mom asked him, his dad standing over them concernedly. Jamie looked around. Everything was normal again. No mysterious blobs, no darkness. The water from the sink was still running, his toothbrush lying on the edge of the sink.

"There- but-" Jamie looked around in shock. "There was stuff," he started. "it was dark and-" Jamie felt as if he couldn't breath. The same empty feeling he felt when those things had been in his room had come over him while he screamed.

"I think you need some rest." his mom answered soothingly as she stood Jamie up.

 His dad walked him to his room. "Get some rest." he playfully ruffled his hair, but the concerned look still showed on his face. Once his dad closed the door, Jamie laid there, staring at the ceiling. This isn't a dream, he thought. Something's happening.

The next day, Jamie left his house early so he could meet up with his friends before he had to go to the station. He found them at Pizza-rama, the most popular pizza place in town. He entered the restaurant and scanned the room for his friends. He spotted them in the corner booth, talking happily to each other. As he approached, they all stopped talking and looked up. Jamie cleared his throat. "Guys, something else happened last night. They aren't dreams. I think whatever is doing this to me is what took Zach." he looked around at his friends. They all looked back at him as if he were crazy.

"Do you hear yourself? You sound ridiculous dude," answered Nicholas honestly.

"I do believe your statement is a bit unbelievable. You would be suggesting that demons and ghosts and different dimensions supposedly were real, when, in reality, they are not." Freddie answered.

"Guys, quit arguing. I think what happened to Zach had made us all a little crazy. Just because what Jamie is saying isn't making a lot of sense to us, doesn't make him crazy. He hasn't even told us what happened." scolded Leslie. The group all leaned back and looked down.

"So what happened Jamie?" questioned Nicholas.

"I don't know how to explain it. I was just in the bathroom brushing my teeth and all of the sudden these weird slug-like blobs appeared." The group made faces and squirmed uncomfortably. "Then," Jamie continued. "it got really dark. Like all the lights had just gone out. Then these weird things started appearing on the wall and this really terrible feeling came over me like it did when I heard those voices in my room. Then my parents came in and it all disappeared and everything went back to normal. They said I just needed more rest. But I know it's real and as crazy as it sounds, it really happened." his friends stared blankly at him.

"Ok, Jamie, I think this Zach thing really has messed you up. That can't be possible. You're talking about a different world or dimension or something." Nicholas said.

"I'm going to have to agree with Nicholas, Jamie," Leslie replied softly. "I want to believe you, but, I can't. That type of thing only exists in movies."

"I'm being serious!" exclaimed Jamie, disrupting a few nearby tables. "If you guys don't want to believe me, fine! But i'm going to figure out what's going on and where Zach went." Jamie stormed away from the table, and out the door, leaving his friends and ignoring their calling out to him. He jogged down the street and continued until he got home. He ran up the stairs and into his room and slammed the door. He threw himself on his bed, not wanting to do anything but go back to sleep. His gaze fell on Tommy, the little robot sat limply on his desk. He started to cry. He had built the robot to remember Charlie, but now it just made him sad. He rolled over facing away from Tommy. He knew he didn't have time to lay around, so he got up and walked out the door to head to the station.

When he arrived, there were at least half a dozen police cars surrounding the station. There were officers with worried looks on their faces. Jamie spotted John and ran up to him.

"What's going on?" he asked.

John turned to jamie with a pained look. "We found your friend," he said slowly. Judging by the look on John's face, he knew not to be excited.

"And?" he asked nervously.

"Well, there were some hunters hunting in the forest, and they came across something." John paused. Jamie felt dizzy as he tried to take in what John was telling him. "They said it looked like a kids' body. They contacted us, and we went over to check it out. The kid was brought to the hospital and was confirmed as Zach Peterson. It was pretty recent because it was obvious he hadn't been lying there long. I'm really sorry, Jamie." John gave Jamie a sympathetic look. "But we are still looking for the man who kidnapped him. I'll let you know if we find anything."

John looked at Jamie with sad eyes and then headed back to a group of police officers who were all talking and looking at notebooks. Jamie watched the world spin around him. This can't be, he thought. He turned and ran from the front of the station, tears stinging his eyes. He ran to Nicholas's house, despite being mad at him. He had to tell him. He ran up the sidewalk onto the front porch and banged on the door. He heard footsteps inside the house, and the door opened.

"Jamie?" questioned Nicholas, surprised.

"He's dead!" exclaimed Jamie, breathing hard.

"What?" asked Nicholas, who was clearly confused.

"I just got back from the station. I was going to ask him about the case. There was a lot of people and police cars there, so I figured something was wrong. I talked to John, some hunters found Zach dead in the woods. He's dead!" Jamie screamed.

Nicholas eyes widened and he looked shocked. "Are you serious?" he searched Jamie's face for a sign that he was joking.

"Yes." was all Jamie said. They walked together down the street towards Leslie's house. They hesitated, then knocked on the door. The door opened, and Leslie's mom appeared.

"Hello, Nicholas, Jamie," she said smiling. They did their best to smile back. "what can I do for you?" she questioned.

"We were looking for Leslie," answered Nicholas quietly.

"I figured," she replied. "she should be home by two. She had a rehearsal for dance."

"Thanks." both boys said, walking back down the steps.

"What do you want to do now?" asked Nicholas glumly.

"I know it sounds weird," remarked Jamie. "but I have a feeling Zach isn't dead. There's something weird happening. I think the voices that were in my room are the ones trying to trick us into thinking he's dead. But he's not!"

Nicholas stopped and buried his face in his hands. "Not this again." he moaned.

"Nicholas, I'm being serious. I know I sound insane, but I just have this feeling."

"Jamie, just because you have a feeling about something doesn't mean it's true. I know you don't want to believe Zach is dead, and I think you're tricking your mind into thinking what you want to believe. He's dead Jamie. You just have to accept that. It's hard for all of us, but you just have to accept what's real." Nicholas lectured.

Jamie shook his head, anger bubbling up inside him all over again. He glared at Nicholas. "If you were my true friend, you would believe me." with that Jamie marched down the road, trying his hardest to keep his tears inside him.

Once again, Jamie found himself sitting at his desk,

staring at the little robot. Jamie remembered back when he spent most of the time at the hospital with Charlie. He remembered him telling Jamie not to be sad, the few times he caught him crying in the little bathroom in the corner of the room, with only room for a tiny bathtub, toilet, and sink smashed together. He remembered the smell of the hospital, a mix of alcohol and sickness. The room was dark, with grey walls and only a small window where a little bit of light would shine through. He remembered his last moments with Charlie. He was holding his hand on the edge of the bed, crying as he listened to the heart monitor drop. The last words Charlie had said to him, even after all these years, had stuck with him, and helped him through a lot in his life. Don't be sad Jamie, I don't want you to cry. You have to be strong for me. The words repeated over and over in his head, making him realize he needed to go back and talk to Nicholas. Charlie had always been a happy kid, always forgiving people if they made a mistake. Even in his last days, he always smiled. Jamie knew that Charlie would want him to make things right with Nicholas, and he didn't want to let him down. Jamie stood up, and before he could change his mind, went out to find Nicholas.

After searching for around half an hour, Jamie found him sitting under an oak staring at what appeared to be nothing.

"Hey," Jamie said embarrassedly, walking over and sitting down next to him. He followed his gaze and stared up at the clouds.

"Hey," replied Nicholas, clearly not over what had

happened earlier.

"I'm sorry about lashing out earlier, and for not being very nice the past few days. Sometimes my emotions overtake me and things get crazy." Jamie paused to look over at Nicholas, who was still looking at the sky. He continued. "I know it doesn't make sense, but I promise I'm not crazy-"

"I know you're not." Nicholas interrupted unexpectedly.

"What?" questioned Jamie, caught off guard.

"Listen. I haven't been completely honest with you. Things have been happening to me too, but I just didn't want to believe it. You mentioning the same type of thing happening to you made me get defensive because I didn't want to believe it." Nicholas nervously glanced at Jamie, who was staring at him in shock.

"Wait, the voices- you heard them too?"

"Yeah. I heard them one day when I was outside watching my little sisters. They had a cold, raspy voice like you said. They were saying how they were going to get us, whatever that meant. I blew it off until something else happened."

"What?" asked Jamie, still in shock.

"I was in this really long hallway, never-ending, it seemed. I started walking and then running. These voices were chasing me, laughing. I ran faster and faster, but the voices got louder and closer. Weird vines started showing up on the walls, and just when it sounded like they were going to get me, it ended. I was sitting on the porch, just like I had been before it happened. My sisters were still playing like they hadn't noticed anything. I decided to not think much about it until you told me the other day about the voices and the bathroom thing."

"Wow," Jamie remarked. "what do you think it is?" Jamie looked anxious as he waited for Nicholas to answer.

"I don't know." was all he could say.

The question Jamie had been wanting to ask him finally came out. "Do you think Zach is really dead?"

Nicholas looked Jamie in the eyes. "No." he replied.

CHAPTER 6

"What do you think we should tell Les and Freddie?" asked Jamie as he and Nicholas crossed the street. He hadn't got much sleep last night, due to everything that had happened the day before.

"The truth," answered Nicholas as they turned the corner onto Leslie's street. "They need to know everything. Maybe they can help us."

"Help us with what?" wondered Jamie.

"With finding Zach and figuring out what's going on."

They walked up to the front door and knocked. This time, Leslie came to the door, her hair pulled back in a ponytail.

"Hey, guys, what's up?" She looked from Jamie to Nicholas.

"We need to talk." Nicholas said.

They walked through the grass, towards the place they knew no one could hear them or see them.

"Where are we going?" Leslie didn't look happy about having to walk through the tall grass.

"Over there." Nicholas pointed to the oak tree they had

sat under yesterday. With Nicholas in the lead, Jamie and Leslie followed behind. They all sat in a circle underneath the tree, a worried look on Leslie's face.

"What's going on?" she asked.

Nicholas took a deep breath. "Ok, so you know how Jamie was talking about voices he heard in his room, and how he saw things in the bathroom?" he asked Leslie.

"Yeah…" she answered slowly.

"Well, they've been happening to me too. But I didn't want to think it was anything, so I didn't pay much attention to it."

Nicholas explained everything he had explained to Jamie the day before, including Zach's "death". When he was finished, Leslie had the same reaction Jamie had had the day before.

"Really?" She asked, looking frightened. "What is it? Is Zach really dead?"

"We don't know," replied Jamie. "The only thing we know is something bad is going on and if we don't do anything about it, it could get a lot worse."

They walked back through the grass and onto the street.

"What do we need to do first?" asked Jamie.

"Well, there's this really strange lady on the end of my street," Leslie remarked. "Everyone thinks that she's a witch, and I've heard she has a lot of weird things in her house."

Jamie and Nicholas exchanged looks.

"Well, I guess that's a start." Jamie said. They headed back to Leslie's house.

"Meet me here at one tomorrow." she told the boys before closing the door.

The next day, Nicholas and Jamie arrived at Leslie's house a few minutes before one. A couple of minutes later, the door opened, and Leslie stepped out.

"Ok," she said. "She lives in that house down there." She pointed down the street to a dark house that looked as if it had been there for hundreds of years. There was moss growing up the side of its black walls, and vines several feet tall stood in the front yard, as if it hadn't been mowed in years. The whole area surrounding the house seemed to be dark.

"Yeesh," said Jamie, shivering.

Nicholas looked at Leslie. "We're going down there?" he asked her with his eyebrows raised. "Hey, you never know. I've heard she knows a lot about supernatural things like this. She could be very helpful."

Jamie and Nicholas exchanged nervous looks. They started down the road towards her house.

"Do you even know her name?" asked Nicholas.

"Well I guess we're about to find out," she replied unfazed, leading them closer towards the house. Nicholas sighed.

"How do you know she's not some maniac killer that eats children for dinner in her weird potions?" asked Jamie, gulping as they neared the place.

Leslie rolled her eyes. "I'm sure she isn't that bad. Besides, I never said she made potions."

"But witches make potions!" exclaimed Jamie.

 "I never said she was a witch either." Leslie seemed amused by the boy's' fear of the woman. When they finally reached the house, there were at least a dozen cats staring at them from the overgrown lawn. Their beady green eyes followed them as they started to walk up what used to be the sidewalk.

"She's a cat lady!" Nicholas yelled in horror.

"I bet she feeds them the body parts of the children she makes in the potion," commented Jamie, turning pale.

 "Guys quit being babies. Some people like cats."

They were almost halfway up the path when a cat crossed by with something dangling from its mouth.

"I told you!" screamed Jamie. "It has a body part in its mouth!"

Leslie chuckled. "I'm pretty sure that was a toy, Jamie."

They reached the steps to the porch, which was overtaken

with cats in all colors and sizes. They meowed and rubbed against the legs of the group. Jamie was trying his hardest not to scream, while Nicholas attempted to escape the four-legged beasts. Somehow managing to get past the cats, Leslie stood confidently in front of the door. She raised her hand to knock.

"Wait!" exclaimed Jamie.

"What?" asked Leslie annoyedly.

"So you're just gonna knock?" he asked.

"What am I supposed to do, just barge in?" Leslie questioned sarcastically. Just as she finished, the big, wooden door swung open. They all spun around and gasped. Standing at the door, was a tall lady with a ruffled gown that went down to her feet. Surprisingly, she didn't have a pointy nose or any witch-like features at all for that matter. She looked from Leslie to Jamie, to Nicholas, who stared back at her silently as they looked one another over. Finally, the woman stepped outside, stroking a cat they hadn't noticed that blended in with her robe.

"May I help you?" she asked, her voice unexpectedly nice.

"Umm-" Nicholas started.

"We were wondering if you could help us with something." Leslie chimed in.

"Why sure!" she exclaimed with almost too much enthusiasm.

"Should we trust her?" whispered Jamie to Leslie, as the

woman was already heading back inside.

"Yes, she's fine." Leslie answered with confidence. They entered the mansion-like house. There were books covering almost every wall and dozens of cats everywhere. The couches, rugs, beds and even the floor were covered in cats. They followed the woman into a small room that had a small table and a lamp.

"Mind my ignorance," Nicholas started. "but how many cats do you have?" Leslie and Jamie stifled a laugh. They hadn't heard Nicholas try to be so proper and polite in a long time.

The woman smiled. "I'm sorry I forgot to mention that! I have 49 in total. Sometimes I get lonely so they help with that."

She bent down and stroked one's head. It arched its back and purred.

"How do you take care of them all?" asked Jamie. "I mean, that has to be a lot of food and, well, money."

The woman laughed. "Well-" she paused, and looked at Jamie, indicating she didn't know his name yet.

"Jamie," he stated. "these are my friends Leslie and Nicholas. He pointed to them, and they smiled.

"Very well," replied the woman cheerfully. "I'm Lucinda. Well anyways, Jamie, when you live all by yourself you don't have much else to do. That's why no one's visits. They all think I'm some witch that has a bunch of cats."

She pets the cat that she had been carrying when she invited them in. Jamie and Nicholas exchanged guilty looks. Leslie looked at them with the 'I told you so' look.

Lucinda stood back up and adjusted the sleeve of her robe. "So, what did you guys need me for? Kids like you usually don't come around here for no reason." she gave a joking smile. The boys turned to Leslie.

 "Well," began Leslie. "I know you're probably going to think we're crazy, but we need some help or advice on some supernatural things that have been happening to me and my friends, it includes a disappearance and supposedly fake death of one of our other friends." Leslie stopped and looked at Lucinda for a sign. Lucinda nodded and stood there for a second with her hand on her chin. Leslie continued. "All of us have been experiencing weird things. Things that can't really be explained." Leslie stopped. Lucinda suddenly puts her hand down and briskly walked over to one of the many bookcases. She scanned over a few rows until she came across a thick red book.

 "Aha!" she exclaimed with excitement. The group crowded around Lucinda as she pulled the book out. She blew on it, and dust flew everywhere. They coughed, then followed Lucinda back into the room they had just come from.

"What is that?" asked Jamie curiously. Leslie and Nicholas looked confusedly over Lucinda's shoulder.

 "This is a book. But not just any book, it's a book called, The Other Side. She turned the book towards Jamie, and in gold letters across the front, it clearly read, The Other

Side.

"What's the other side?" questioned Jamie.

"It's what I believe you're experiencing," answered Lucinda casually. Seeing the confused looks on the kids' faces, she began to explain. "Two hundred fifty years ago exactly, the town of Branford experienced weird disappearances. No one could explain it. And it wasn't just one person, oh no, it was thirty."

"Thirty!" exclaimed Nicholas.

Lucinda nodded. "They were there one moment and gone the next. Nobody knew why. Anyone who was close to the people who went missing, or anyone who were family members of people close to the person who went missing, experienced strange things. Indescribable things."

"I and Jamie have been experiencing weird things." Nicholas said quietly.

Lucinda nodded again. "After five days, the missing person would be proclaimed dead. It was always something different. But then, there was one man, named Alistair Poncho, who was curious to figure out what was really going on. Just like you, he knew the people weren't really dying. He was determined to figure out what was really going on. The whole town thought it was just a hoax, so they made fun of Alistair for thinking it was something bigger and darker, which they didn't want to believe. Fast forward a few months, Alistair had finally got a lead. There was this weird circle he noticed at the edge of the town. One day, Alistair was studying the circle when it made a noise and flashed. He went to touch it, but instead of feeling a solid circle, his hand went through, to the other side. Several days later, he decided to go through to the other side and found hideous things. Things that crawled and crept. Dark, slender monsters with demon eyes. It wasn't safe in the circle. Long story short, the man discovered they had been taking the missing people. They tried to trick the town into thinking they were dead, so they could take over the town and eventually the world. It was never found out how they went away, or why. All we know is that they vanished, as did Alistair. No one ever saw him again. The town has forgotten about this time, except for me. And it appears to be happening again." Lucinda sighed. "Is that all you wanted to know?' she questioned, examining the kids' reactions.

"Uh, yes, thank you." said Nicholas, who had gone completely pale.

"We'd better get going," Leslie answered, looked nervous. "If this is what you think it is, I guess we'll be seeing you soon."

They said their goodbyes and filed single file out the door and through the tangled weeds.

Once they were all out on the road and several yards away from the house, they all exchanged frightened glances.

"Do you think she could be right?" asked Nicholas.

"She seemed pretty legit," responded Jamie, trying to act normal.

Leslie was being unnaturally quiet, walking with her hands in her pockets and her head down. "I'm sorry guys," she said quietly.

"For what?" asked Jamie and Nicholas together.

"For taking you guys there. I'm pretty sure she was taking advantage of us "little kids" because she knew we would believe her if she told us some dumb made up story." Leslie kicked a rock down the road and continued walking.

"But what if it wasn't some dumb made up story?" Nicholas asked Leslie. "What if it's true?" Leslie stopped walking. "Don't be ridiculous!" scoffed Leslie.

"You're the one who brought us there in the first place!" Nicholas snapped back.

"Guys!" exclaimed Jamie. They both stopped, then with angry faces continued down the road.

Once they had made it back to Leslie's house, Leslie walked up to her front lawn, without saying goodbye. Nicholas huffed in Leslie's direction, glaring towards the front door.

"Don't get mad at her. She's just mad because she didn't hear what she wanted to hear." Jamie started walking back towards his house.

"What did she want to hear?" questioned Nicholas, catching up to Jamie.

"Probably not that there's some portal that sucks people up and never returns them," responded Jamie.

Nicholas nodded in agreement. "It sounds pretty crazy, but do you think that's what it is?" he asked.

"It sounds like it," Jamie answered. "I guess we need to figure it out and then go back to Lucinda's."

By the time Jamie had walked Nicholas home, the moon was already out. It glowed through the cloudy sky, giving off a rather creepy color surrounding Jamie. He shivered as the night wind chilled him. He turned the corner onto the street which should have been his, except it wasn't there. Jamie frowned. He looked around. To the right, was Maple Street. To the left, was Wall Street. He began to panic. His street had always been in between those streets. Where was it now? He started walking down the road that was once his. In place of the road where the pavement once was, was a thick, black liquid that came up to Jamie's knees. He pushed forward, although the black liquid tried to hold him back. In place of all the houses, were piles of rubble that were at least a story tall each. Fog filled the remaining places. The whole area was a dark grey and had no color. Jamie looked around nervously. He didn't understand. Where had all of this come from? Suddenly a voice rang out. Don't go home Jamie, it said, in a deep, raspy voice. Jamie spun around searching for the voice. "Who are you?" he shouted. Don't go home Jamie, it repeated. There is something very unpleasant there waiting for you. It cackled, sending chills down Jamie's spine. Jamie began running, fighting the gooey substance underneath him. The noise chased him, getting louder and louder. He stopped and squeezed his eyes closed, and began to sink into the thick dark substance. When he opened his eyes, everything was normal. He was standing in the middle of his street, which actually looked like his street. He looked down at his feet, but there were no dark stains anywhere. Just as Jamie was calming down, he noticed something going on in his house. Dread washed over Jamie, remembering what the voice had said. But that wasn't real, he thought confusedly. As Jamie looked closer, he saw a figure rushing frantically around the house, entering new rooms, flipping light switches on and off. Jamie jogged up to his house and nervously opened the door. To his horror, he saw his mom sprawled out on the floor in a very uncomfortable position. "Mom!" Jamie ran over to her and sat down next to her. Jamie gasped when he saw her stone grey face and black eyes staring back at him. Her veins popped out, and she appeared to not be able to breathe as if someone were strangling her. Slowly rushing the life out of her innocent body. Grabbing at her throat, Jamie noticed that the same slug-like thing that had been in the sink was now slithering out of his mother's throat. Jamie screamed and jumped back, just as it crept out of her mouth, disappearing into thin air. He turned around to look for his dad and bumped into him as he was running out of the living room. "What's happening?" asked Jamie, as everything around him became blurry.

"I don't know," answered his dad, panicked. "I called 911, they should be here anytime." his dad rushed over to his mom who was still laying on the floor. He wrapped his arms around her and told her it would be ok. Tears blurred Jamie's vision. He ran up to his room. He curled up on his bed and cried, as sirens sounded outside of his house. He listened as the police entered his house, he heard the clacking of the movable bed he had never learned the name of, even after Charlie had used it. He heard the slam of the ambulance doors and listened as the screeching sirens faded into the nighttime air. Everything played in slow motion. Jamie's head was spinning, the silence of the house made Jamie feel alone. He laid on his bed, not moving. Then, out of the dark silence of the shadows in the corner of his room, he heard a faint, deep voice. *I warned you, Jamie, I warned you.*

CHAPTER 7

Jamie stared at his mom as she slept peacefully in the hospital bed. Her face had returned somewhat to normal, and her heart was beating at a steady rate. There were tubes everywhere. Stuck in her arms, attached to her face, and even one on her leg. Little "stickers" as the doctors' had explained to him as were stuck on her chest with little tubes in them connected to a heart machine. This room was almost all white, nothing like when he had been here with Charlie. The walls were white, the floor was white, there were white paintings, and even his mother's hospital gown was white. He watched her sleep, hoping she would wake up soon. His dad was sleeping in a chair close to the window. Jamie sat impatiently in another chair, close to his mother's bed. He noticed her eyes were surrounded in a dark grey color, and she seemed different. He didn't know what it was, but he could sense she was different somehow. A nurse knocked on the door, and then entered the room. Jamie never got why they even knocked, because they never waited for an answer anyways. A petite nurse walked in. Her chocolate brown hair swung in a little ponytail that couldn't have been longer than a couple of inches. She had glasses and was carrying a clipboard underneath her left arm. She smiled warmly at Jamie as she headed towards his mom's bed. She adjusted the heart machine, and watched it closely for a second. "Is everything alright?" Jamie asked concernedly. The nurse spun around, startled by his question.

"What?" she asked him, caught off guard.

"Is everything ok?" Jamie repeated.

"Oh, yeah," she responded with a small chuckle. "I was just checking her levels. She seems to be doing pretty well." she shot a glance towards his mother.

"But what happened last night," started Jamie. "is that normal?"

The nurse pressed her lips together. "Medical issues can cause many things to happen to the human body. It may not seem normal, but if certain things don't function properly, it can cause some pretty weird things to happen. Some worse than others." The nurse gave Jamie a forced smile and turned to walk out the door. Once the door closed, Jamie sat back in his seat, staring at his mom angrily. He knew what had happened last night wasn't normal. He knew it had to do something with whatever was going on in Branford. He remembered Lucinda saying that anyone who was close to the people who went missing would experience weird things. He sighed. He wish he could tell his parents what was happening. But he knew they wouldn't believe him. Now his dad wouldn't know what happened to his mom, and the doctor's wouldn't be able to find out what happened, because nothing that can be explained by doctors had happened. It was those things. Those creepy, nasty things that haunted him. Trying to ruin his life and everyone around him.

"Jamie!" he heard a voice shout from across the room. He

quickly looked up, noticing his dad looking at him.

"Yeah?" asked Jamie.

"Are you ok?" he questioned, looking concerned.

"Oh, yeah, I'm fine," Jamie looked over at his mom. "Is she going to wake up soon?"

Jamie's dad pressed his lips together, like the nurse had done moments ago. "I don't know, Jamie," he answered. "The doctor said she was in a coma and that they would try to wait for her, but they can't wait forever." His dad turned his gaze towards her, sleeping peacefully in her bed, oblivious to what was going on around her. Jamie didn't know what caused it, but suddenly he had an aching pain in his heart. Looking at his mom, knowing how little time he had had with her. Remembering Charlie, and how he had died so young. His family was falling apart. He let out a small screech, and with no way to stop them, tears flooded his face. He leaned back in his chair, and continued to cry. There was no way to stop them. They kept coming and coming. His dad stood up and dragged a chair from the other side of the room over next to Jamie. He sat down and wrapped his arm around him. Once Jamie had stopped crying, they both sat there in silence and stared at his mom. "She looks beautiful, doesn't she?" said his dad, breaking the silence.

"Yeah." answered Jamie smiling.

"We have to stay hopeful," his dad said, patting Jamie on the shoulder. "that she'll wake up soon." Jamie nodded, trying hard not to meet his dad's gaze.

Jamie quickly walked through the hospital doors, excited to get some fresh air, and escape the place that always made him feel tense and afraid. He told his dad he was going to Nicholas's house, which wasn't exactly a lie. He was going to tell Nicholas what had happened, and then go back to Lucinda's, because now he knew that something wasn't right, and Lucinda was the only person who could help them now.

Jamie banged on the door to the Fulkerson's house, too impatient to wait. He heard footsteps inside, and then the door opened. "Hey Jamie, what's up?" Nicholas stepped outside, closing the door behind him.

"We need to go back to Lucinda's." Jamie stated.

"What?" questioned Nicholas.

"We need to go to Lucinda's," Jamie repeated. "Something bad happened to my mom last night and she's in a coma. C'mon." Jamie turned and headed down the sidewalk.

Bewildered, Nicholas followed. "Your mom's in a coma?" he asked in disbelief.

"Yeah," Jamie said, looking down at the freshly paved road. "the doctors' don't know if she's going to come out." he took a deep breath.

"Wow. I'm really sorry, Jamie. What happened?"

"Those things. The ones we've been seeing. They attacked her or something. It was terrible." They continued walking towards the house they had once been afraid of.

"Are we going to Leslie's?" asked Nicholas as they neared her house.

"No," answered Jamie sharply. "You know she doesn't believe us. You heard what she said yesterday."

Nicholas nodded in agreement. "Yeah." he said.

"Are we going to tell Freddie about all of this? He hasn't even heard about Lucinda. He's been away on that thing for algebra club or something."

Nicholas made a face. "I can't believe he does math for fun." he said shivering.

Jamie chuckled. "He's definitely different. But that's what I like about him, even if he's annoying sometimes."

They stopped in front of the dark, barren house. As usual, cats sat in the yard, staring at them with their glowing eyes as they stepped up onto the sidewalk.

"Those cats still give me the creeps." Nicholas said, staring back into their beady eyes. They once again approached the porch leading into the old woman's house. Jamie knocked on the door, more confident this time. The door swung open, and Lucinda appeared, wearing what seemed to be the same black robe she had worn before. She raised her eyebrows, looking surprised to see them. She smiled. "Well, I wasn't expecting you so soon!" She gestured at them to come inside. They walked inside the mansion, the familiar smell of cats and mold filled the air. They walked into the small room where she had shown them the book. They all sat down, and a black cat jumped onto Lucinda's lap. "So, what brings you back? And where is your little friend?" Lucinda's face straightened and she crossed her hands in front of her, ready to listen.

"Well, Leslie couldn't make it today," began Jamie. "but we're back because those things, that are talking to Nicholas and me, they came back. They did something to · my mom. She's in a coma in the hospital, and the doctor's don't know if they can bring her back."

A serious expression spread over Lucinda's face. "Hmm. I'm really sorry about your mom. She will probably wake up, because the Jinn's like to torture the people close to the victim rather than kill." Lucinda paused.

"What's a Jinn?" asked Jamie.

"Jinn's are the things you and your friend are experiencing. They are the "workers" I guess you could call them of their master, the one who wants to take over the world. He uses them to get what he wants. The people that live in our universe." Lucinda stopped.

"Who is their master?" questioned Jamie.

"We don't need to talk about that now. I was afraid it would come to this. We're going to have to do something. If we don't, things will get much worse, and we will give the master what it wants, our world. Now I'll warn you, it's dangerous. But we can't let them win. We must save our world!" with that, Lucinda got up, the black cat leaping down before it could get knocked off. Nicholas and Jamie watched as she rummaged through the books on one of her many bookcases. She searched down the rows until she found a particularly large book, bigger than the one she had shown them last time. It had a hard green cover and looked to be very ancient. Blowing the dust off of the front, Lucinda flipped quickly through the pages, until she stopped at a page a little past the mid section of the book. She read down the page, and then slammed it shut. "Ok, first we're going to have to locate the circle. I guess you could call it a portal to the other side." Lucinda sat back down in the chair across from the boys.

"So, how do we do that?" asked Nicholas.

"There isn't actually any exact way to find it." answered Lucinda.

"What do you mean by that?" asked Jamie.

 "There isn't anything special we can do to find it. We just have to search around town until we find it." Lucinda was now stroking a different cat that had jumped up on her lap.

"So we just walk around town until we find it?" questioned Jamie.

"Yes," Lucinda replied. "And when you find it, come back here and we'll start the second step." with that Lucinda stood up, and headed towards the door. The boys followed, and stepped out into the chilly fall air. "Now remember, don't do anything else but find the circle. It could be very dangerous if you do otherwise." Lucinda stepped back inside and closed the door. As the boys made their way back to the street, they talked about how they would find the circle.

"Do you think it's somewhere close?" questioned Nicholas.

"I have no idea. This is the craziest thing i've ever done before." Jamie took a deep breath and tucked his hands into his coat pockets.

"When should we start?" Nicholas asked, scanning his eyes around the area.

"Right now." replied Jamie. "We have to stop those things from taking over. It's up to us now. No one else will believe us if we tell them." Jamie remarked. Nicholas nodded in agreement. They continued walking down the road, until they had reached Jamie's house. "We can start here," Jamie stated. "We'll work our way around town." The two boys headed around street by street, not knowing what was lurking there around them.

CHAPTER 8

"We've searched everywhere!" exclaimed Jamie, throwing his hands in the air. He paced around Nicholas's room, while Nicholas sat on the edge of his bed. "We searched downtown, middletown, alleys, the forest! Every inch of this town! It's not here!" Jamie turned towards Nicholas, slapping his hands down by his side.

"I don't know, Jamie. I really don't. Lucinda told us it was here, so it has to be. Maybe we aren't searching good enough." Nicholas opened a bag of Doritos and popped one in his mouth. Jamie flopped down in a chair.

"We've looked everywhere. I don't know where else to look." Jamie defeatedly played with a small hole on the arm of the chair.

"We can't give up," answered Nicholas. "Halloween is less than a week away. Who knows what the Jinn's are planning. Little kids dressed up, running around on the streets. It'll be the perfect time for them to come in and take them. I mean, it's Halloween. Everyone will be in costume, no one will notice them." Nicholas swallowed another mouthful of chips.

"That's the thing. We've only heard them. We've never seen them. How are we supposed to know what they look like?" Jamie asked, tension in his voice.

"We aren't supposed to know that right now." replied Nicholas. "Lucinda told us to only find the portal. Nothing else." Nicholas balled up the chip bag and tossed it into the trash can.

"Well I'm tired," Jamie stated. "I can't sleep in that hospital. My dad said I'm allowed to stay home tonight. So I can sleep." Jamie stood up to leave the room. "I'll see you tomorrow. We can figure something out tomorrow." Jamie headed home quickly, as darkness surrounded him. The only light was from houses, if they even still had their lights on. Jamie unlocked his front door, and headed to his room. He got ready for bed, then laid in his bed, staring at the ceiling. He heard faint whispers coming from the corner. *Skotadi,* it hissed. Over and over again. *Skotadi, skotadi.* Jamie covered his face with the blankets and squeezed his eyes shut. Once the sound faded, Jamie slowly pulled the covers down. He scanned the room, but there was nothing to be seen. He sighed. Rolling onto his side, he faced the window where a stream of light beamed from the moon and shone on his desk, lighting up Tommy. Jamie remembered when he was always working on robots, trying to figure them out. Then Zach went missing, and everything stopped. Jamie rolled back over, to where he stared at the ceiling, the moonlight made it visible enough for him to see the outline of the stars and outer space objects that had once been in place right above his bed. When Charlie died, he had taken them all down. Space had been their thing. They had both wanted to be astronauts. Then one day, Charlie got sick. Jamie remembered his mom trying to calm him down as the ambulances took them both away. His dad had held him back, as Charlie and his mom were taken to the hospital. It was only a matter of weeks before the cancer took over his small 4 year old body, and death whisked him away, leaving 8 year old Jamie and his family. Jamie was determined to find the circle. He couldn't let innocent lives be taken, like his brother's was. He closed his eyes, knowing tomorrow could be the day they would find it.

Jamie woke up to a quiet, empty house. He knew his parents weren't usually home when he got up, but knowing where they were made it feel more empty than usual. He got dressed, then rode his bike to the hospital.

He opened the door to his mom's room, and to his surprise, she was awake! Jamie smiled and ran over to her. He stood in front of her bed, his smile quickly fading. Instead of looking back at Jamie, she was staring at the wall, looking around Jamie. He frowned. "Mom." he said quietly. He waved his hand in front of her face. She didn't respond. Her eyes were glazed over, and her face seemed to have a grayish tint. Her body looked fragile and pale. "M-mom." Jamie stuttered, his voice cracking. He glanced over at his dad, whose face was red from crying. "What happened?" asked Jamie. "What's wrong with her?" Jamie sniffed and wiped the tears from his eyes.

"I don't know, Jamie. She woke up last night, she's been doing that ever since. The doctor's don't know what's wrong with her. She hasn't said a word yet." his dad looked sadly over at his mom. Jamie gave one last look at his mom, then headed for the door. "Jamie!" his dad called after him.

"I have to go somewhere!" Jamie screamed back. He raced down the hallway and out the door. He ran all the way to

Nicholas's house. Nicholas opened the door, and saw Jamie. He frowned. "What's wrong?" he asked.

"My mom. She woke up last night. But she won't respond to us. She won't move. Her face is grey and she looks weak." Jamie tried his best to hold in his tears.

Nicholas's eyes widened. "Let's go to my room." he answered.

The boys sat down on the bed. "Has anything else happened to you?" asked Nicholas.

Jamie nodded. "Last night. I was in bed, and I heard that voice come from the corner again. It was saying "Skotadi". Whatever that means." Jamie pulled a thread hanging off of the bed. "Wait," Nicholas replied, his eyes squinting. "Skotadi?"

Jamie nodded. Nicholas whispered something under his breath. He suddenly shot his head up. "Dark!" he said finally.

"Huh?" Jamie questioned confusedly.

"Skotadi means dark in Greek!" Nicholas exclaimed.

"Since when do you know Greek?" scoffed Jamie.

Nicholas rolled his eyes. "My mom made me study it, okay?" Nicholas adjusted his position on the bed. "I think it was trying to tell us something. Give us a hint. Maybe it means that it's dark where the circle is!" Nicholas leaped off the bed.

Jamie frowned. "Where is it dark at? The only darkness I know is nighttime." Jamie stated. Nicholas shook his head. "No," he replied. "there's another place that's dark. It's the only place we haven't looked!" Nicholas looked hopeful at Jamie.

Jamie shook his head. "I don't get it." he replied.

"Lucinda's! Duh! It's super dark and creepy in their. Where else could it be?"

The boys looked at each other. "Well what are we waiting for? Let's go!"

Jamie and Nicholas darted out the door and raced down the street, bumping straight into Leslie. They all fell in a pile, then quickly stood up, looking one another over.

"What are you guys doing here?" Leslie asked, smirking at them.

"We're going to Lucinda's." Nicholas said quickly. Before Leslie could respond, Nicholas continued, lowering his voice. "The other night, those things, they're called Jinn's, did something to Jamie's mom and put her in a coma, so we went back to Lucinda's and she told us we needed to locate the portal. We searched all day, but we couldn't find it. Last night, Jamie heard the Jinn's whispering "Skotadi" which is Greek for dark. Lucinda's house is dark, and it's the only place we haven't looked. This morning Jamie went to check on his mom and she won't move or do anything." Nicholas looked at Leslie with pleading eyes. "Please, Come with us. We'll do this together." They both looked at Leslie intently. Leslie moved her eyes from

Nicholas to Jamie, a blank look on her face.

She swallowed. "Ok," she answered confidently. "Let's go." The boys smiled and looked happily at each other. "C'mon!" exclaimed Leslie, already several feet in front of them. "We have a portal to find."

Lucinda answered the door, and smiled when she saw them. "Back again, are we?" she said in her airy, pleasant voice.

"We think the portal is here." Jamie stated sharply.

Puzzled, Lucinda opened the door wider. "Here? In my house?" she continued to look bewildered as she led them all into her home.

"Yes." Jamie said.

They all began searching the whole downstairs, but found nothing. They continued onto the second floor, but again, there was nothing different about it. The group made their way into the attic and searched the rather large room. Cobwebs flooded the room, which was covered in dust and musty furniture. They began to split into sections of the room, crossing over the creaky wooden floors. Nicholas made his way to a dusty corner in the room. He looked closely at the corner. Seeing nothing, he started to turn and walk away. Just then, a small *whoosh* noise coming from behind him caught his attention. Turning back to the corner, he noticed a glass-like film covering the corner and the surrounding areas. It was about the length of a door. He examined it closer, then stuck his hand out near it. It made a buzz, and the movement from his hand made it ripple all the way across the film. "Guys," Nicholas called. "I think I found something." The others gathered around Nicholas to stare at his discovery.

"That's definitely it." Lucinda said in disbelief. "That's the circle."

They all gazed in awe at the circle.

"We must go," Lucinda remarked at once. "It's not safe to be around it right now." Lucinda turned and started heading back down the stairs.

"Wow," Leslie answered. "You guys were right." The friends continued admiring the portal until Lucinda called to them once again.

"Children, come on, we have work to do."

Once they were back downstairs, Lucinda led the group towards the door.

"Wait, you're making us leave? We just found the circle!" Nicholas whined.

"Yes, I know," Lucinda replied matter of factly. "There are certain things that must be done first in order to achieve what we are doing. Certain circumstances that must first be met. I should be done preparing by tomorrow. Meet me here and we will discuss the first operation." Lucinda smiled as she pushed the children out the door, gently closing it behind her.

The group walked side by side back down the street.

"I can't believe we actually found it." Jamie remarked surprisingly.

"I know. I was starting to think there wasn't one." Nicholas replied.

Leslie walked with her hands in her pockets, looking slightly down at the ground. Her blonde hair was pulled back in braids, and it seemed to glow in the sunlight, blinding anyone who looked at it for too long. She looked up. "I'm sorry about what I said the other day," she finally said. "It wasn't very nice. But I mean it's kind of hard to believe a crazy lady with a bunch of cats at the end of the street, telling us a story about some portal leading to another world with monsters." She gave a small smile.

"But I guess it's true," Nicholas said. "There really is a portal. We just saw it. Do you really think that's what's happening to your mom?" Nicholas looked over at Jamie.

"It has to be," he answered. "Nothing else could make her do that. You heard what Lucinda said. She said the Jinn's could affect anyone who knew Zach. Maybe if we can get rid of the portal again, everything will return to normal. Zach will be back, and we can be normal kids again." Jamie looked hopefully back at Lucinda's. The group continued walking until they had reached Jamie's house.

"You gonna be at school tomorrow?" questioned Nicholas.

"I don't know, probably not. My parents don't really care right now. Are you?" Jamie was more so asking both of them.

"My mom said I didn't have to because of all the Zach stuff going on. I think she's taking harder than me." Nicholas and Leslie were still lingering outside of his house.

"Probably because she doesn't know what we do. Everyone in town besides us thinks that Zach is dead." Leslie chimed in.

They all nodded in agreement. "Well I'll see you tomorrow, Jamie." Nicholas turned and walked away.

 "See ya!" Jamie called after him.

 He turned to Leslie. "Has anything happened to you yet?" he asked her.

 "I don't know. I've been having weird nose bleeds and scratches." she pulled up her sleeve to reveal a long scratch that appeared to be infected.

Jamie cringed. "Leslie! Did one of the Jinn's do that?" he looked at her nervously.

She shrugged. "I think so. It just popped up all of the sudden then got infected." she pulled her sleeve back down. "Well I guess I'll see you tomorrow," Leslie sighed. "We can figure things out then." she turned to walk away.

"Goodnight Leslie." Jamie said.

"Goodnight Jamie." Leslie gave a small smile at him then continued down the road until she disappeared into her house. Jamie decided he wanted to go stay with his mom and dad. It felt really empty staying home by himself all night. He rode his bike to the hospital, and spent the night on the little ledge by the window that was in every hospital room. Jamie's mom still hadn't spoken or moved. She was still sitting in the same position as earlier, staring at the same spot on the wall. The bathroom door creaked open, and his dad came out and sat down in his chair. He caught Jamie's eye, and gave him a sad smile. Jamie smiled back, then his dad turned out the lights and they both went to bed.

CHAPTER 9

The next morning, Jamie awoke to doctors surrounding his mom's bed, yelling orders at each other and running around as if they didn't have much time.

"Do you have the defibrillator?" one doctor screamed to another.

The doctor that they had been yelling at ran over with two little paddles. Jamie quickly sat up, and to his horror, they slapped his mom with them. He remembered back when Charlie was dying, how the doctors had smacked him with the shockers, but it hadn't worked. He spotted his dad crying next to a small nurse a few feet away from his mom. It was the same nurse he had talked to a few days ago. Jamie stood up and walked over to his dad. As soon as he got there, a stocky guy doctor walked over to Jamie and started to lead him out of the room.

"What are you doing? That's my mom!" Jamie struggled against the doctor as he seized him by the arms and dragged him away. Tears pouring down his face, he watched as he was being pulled out the door, his mom being shocked over and over again. Her face was pale and her mouth was all the way open. Doctors continued rushing around, attempting everything they could to save her.

Jamie, Nicholas, and Leslie sat under the tree they had sat under when they were first discussing the things that were happening. Except now they were talking about how to fix the things.

"Should we go to Lucinda's?" wondered Nicholas.

Jamie nodded. "We need to ask her if my mom's going to be okay. And besides, we need to know how to stop the Jinn's and their master from taking over the world." Nicholas nodded. "How is she?" Leslie asked in a concerned tone. "I mean your mom. Did they revive her?"

Jamie sighed. "Yeah. They have to keep a close eye on her though. She did almost die."

As they made their way towards Lucinda's, Jamie's phone rang. They all stopped.

"Hello?" Jamie said slowly, as he picked up the phone. The others watched intently. "Oh, um, ok." There was a pause. "Uh, sure, we'll be right there." Another pause. "Yeah, thanks." Jamie hung up the phone and turned to face the others. "John wants us to come in."

As they entered John's office, they sat along the chairs in the same order as usual. As John walked in and closed the door behind them, Jamie could sense something was wrong. John took his seat behind his desk, flipping through some papers. He glanced up with a troubled look on his face.

"So your friend, Frederick Cowl, has been on a school trip

the past few days?" John looked at them for an answer.

"Um, yes, he was in Ohio with the school for a state contest. He was supposed to come home today." as he said it, Jamie realized that Freddie wasn't home.

Apparently thinking the same thing, Nicholas asked, "Is he home? I haven't seen him today." The group exchanged glances.

John took a deep breath. "That's what I wanted to talk to you about. I know he's your good friend, but please keep an open mind and don't get to upset when I tell you this." John looked uncomfortable at the kids. Jamie gulped. Nicholas and Leslie both had nervous looks on their faces.

 "Last night the school reported that Freddie had went missing. They sent out a search team to find him. They located him inside of a school that was in Ohio. They reported him dead as of 7:58 this morning." John looked mournful at the group. "I'm sorry guys." John stood up to leave. "Wait!" exclaimed Jamie, horrified. "You mean Freddie's dead?" he stood up to look John in the eyes.

"I'm sorry kid." he said.

With that he left the room, closing the door behind him. Jamie looked at his friends, who looked just as sad and confused as he did. Jamie furrowed his eyebrows.

"They took Zach, they made my mom sick and who knows if she'll ever be able to talk or move again, and now they've killed Freddie. I know Freddie was our friend, and we should be sad, but we can't let that get in the way of destroying the circle. C'mon guys, we're going to Lucinda's." Before the others could speak, Jamie was already exiting the room and walking towards the door.

Once they had arrived at Lucinda's, she had them busy working on ways to first, trick the Jinn's into going back into the circle, then trapping them in so they could do something that Lucinda hadn't yet explained, to make the circle weak, to where the Jinn's couldn't get back to the other side, but they could. They would then need to enter the circle, which is very dangerous. They would rescue everyone the Jinn's had taken, then put some type of trap on the circle, triggering a weakness in the master. Once the master was gone, there wouldn't be anything left, and everything would return to normal. Of course, it was easier said than done. Entering the circle would be life threatening. If everything wasn't planned perfect, they would die. If everything didn't work perfect, they would die. If they forgot or left out anything, the would die. Which was why Lucinda was training them so hard. Four hours later, they had finally finished learning how to lure the Jinn's inside. Lucinda read the directions in the book, then they would all plan it out on a piece of paper, sketching what they had to do for it to work. They figured out they would have to send one of them as bait, to get the master's attention. If the master noticed one of them, he would call the Jinn's to come and get him. The master never left the circle, so in order to receive his request of who he needed them to get, the Jinn's would have to go into the circle to the master. Once they went into the circle, the person sent as bait would have to cover the opening to the circle with saran wrap, then sprinkle a mixture of salt and vinegar on top in a thin layer. This was said to keep the Jinn's from escaping the circle again. "So, that means they won't be able to torture us anymore?" questioned Jamie hopefully.

"If everything goes as planned." remarked Lucinda, shutting the book and placing it back on the bookcase. She returned to the table, where Jamie, Nicholas, and Leslie sat, tired from the hours of thinking they had done.

"Meet me here tomorrow at no later than four. This usually works best at night, so they can't see our bait as well."

Nicholas looked from Lucinda to Jamie to Leslie. "Well who's gonna be the bait?" he asked, trying not to sound nervous.

"Me," Jamie answered quickly.

They all turned to look at him. "You *want* to be the bait?" Leslie asked him, her eyebrows raised slightly.

"Are you sure, dear? It's very dangerous." Lucinda said in her soft voice, it quivered a bit at the end.

"Yes. I want to show those Jinn's who's boss." Jamie held his head confidently in the air.

"Unless they show you who's boss first, when they tear your head off and rip you into thousands of pieces and leave us without a bait." Nicholas said sarcastically.

"Now boys, that's enough. I'll see you at four tomorrow?" she looked at Jamie and Nicholas. They nodded. "Very well, then. Come prepared." Lucinda led them out of the house, as usual. "Yeah, prepared to die." Nicholas muttered under his breath, only loud enough that Jamie heard it.

"So, now what do we do?" asked Leslie as they made their way home.

"I guess we go home and get some sleep. We have a big day tomorrow. The world could be on the line if we mess it up." Jamie watched his breath float up into the air in a little puff of white. "And family." Nicholas added.

"And friends." Leslie said.

Jamie walked Nicholas and Leslie home, then he headed back to his empty house. He had decided it would be best if he stayed away from the hospital tonight. Besides, the little ledge by the window was really hard and cold and he hadn't slept well on it.

He laid in bed, wondering if the circle really would trap the Jinn's inside, if he completed his task. The Jinn's had taken two of his good friends, and made his mom sick. How could he not want to be the one to trap them? He knew it was dangerous, and if he messed up he could die, but it was worth it if it saved their town and world in the end. He just hoped he could do everything right.

<u>CHAPTER 10</u>

The next day, Jamie woke up later than usual. He looked over at his clock, which read ten o'clock. He jumped out of bed and ran over to his window. Below he saw his friends standing on the front porch. He quickly got dressed, then went outside to meet them. They all turned to look at him as he opened the door.

"Slept in today, huh?" Nicholas answered, amused.

"How long have you guys been here?" Jamie squinted at them trying to see them through the blinding sun.

"Probably around forty-five minutes or so," answered Leslie. "We wanted to do some reviewing on what we need to do tonight."

The group headed towards their usual spot, the oak tree. They all crowded in under it, Leslie taking out the binder Lucinda had gave her with their plan. Leslie opened the binder, and flipped through some pages.

"Ok," she started. "So Jamie, you're going to be our bait, so you need to be walking around outside Lucinda's house at about seven o'clock. The master will see you alone, so he will want the Jinn's to get you and bring you to their world, which would be either killing you or taking you. The master will call the Jinn's into the circle so he can tell them what to do to you, which is where another one of us will be hiding somewhere in the room with the portal, so we can tell you when they go in." Leslie paused to let all of it sink in, then continued. "Once the Jinn's cross into the circle, the person in the attic with the portal will tell you, and you need to go inside the house and grab the saran wrap, salt, and vinegar. You and the person in the attic need to cross the saran wrap over the circle entrance then mix the salt and vinegar together so you can sprinkle it on the saran wrap. All of this needs to be done within fifteen minutes, or the master will be done talking to the Jinn's and he will notice you and kill you." Leslie closed the binder. "Got it?" she gave a serious look towards Jamie.

He swallowed. "Got it." he answered back.

"Ok," Leslie said. "If this works, then we can move on to step two. But if it doesn't, that's the end for all of us. Nicholas, either you or me are going to have to be in the room with the portal. Lucinda and whoever isn't going to be there will be on guard in the house." Leslie looked over at Nicholas.

"Um…" Nicholas started. "I guess I'll be in the attic. You can stay on patrol with Lucinda." Nicholas gave a nervous look at Leslie.

"Great," Leslie clapped her hands together. "We should be done with the entire thing by ten. We'll have to stay over at Lucinda's for awhile until we know it worked."

When it was four o'clock, they all walked over to

Lucinda's to prepare for their big night.

"Ok," Lucinda said excitedly, "I'll go get the saran wrap, you guys mix the salt and vinegar up in that large bowl that's under the sink." Lucinda disappeared into the next room, as Leslie and Jamie mixed the salt and vinegar into the bowl. Nicholas sat on the floor a few feet away from them, playing with the cats with a string that had a feather attached to the end. Jamie smiled at him.

"The cats aren't so bad after all, huh?" he said teasingly to Nicholas.

Nicholas glared at him. "I'm just distracting them from you guys. They would knock over everything." Nicholas continued dragging the string around on the floor, the cats attempting to pounce on the feather. Jamie rolled his eyes and continued mixing. Just then, Lucinda returned with a thing of saran wrap.

"Are you guys finished?" she asked, peering over their shoulders at the gritty vinegar in their bowl.

She smiled. "Excellent." she remarked.

They carried the supplies up to the attic, where they sat it in the corner and threw a blanket over top of it. They looked over at the clock. It read six o'clock.

"One more hour." Jamie said. They all glanced around at each other, nervous looks taking over their faces.

"It's time!" exclaimed Lucinda, just as the clock read seven. They switched out all of the lights. Lucinda and Leslie ran over by the window in the kitchen which looked out over the front of the house. Nicholas went upstairs, giving Jamie a thumbs up. Jamie took a deep breath. *It's all or nothing,* he thought to himself. He made his way to the road in front of Lucinda's house, the night air chilling him. He pretended to be going down the street, looking around at the scenery. Ten more minutes passed, but nothing happened. Just as Jamie was turning around, he saw Nicholas giving his signal through the attic window. Jamie raced back to the house, greeted by Leslie and Lucinda.

"They're here," Leslie whispered. "Good luck."

They walked back into the kitchen. Jamie bravely walked up the stairs to the attic, where he met Nicholas.

"They just walked through the portal," he whispered. "C'mon. We don't have much time."

The boys silently ran over to their supplies. They took off the cover, and grabbed the saran wrap.

"You hold this end and I'll stretch it over the opening." Nicholas thrust the package at Jamie. They stretched it over the portal, smoothing down the sides. "Ok, go get the salt." Nicholas whispered to Jamie. Jamie ran over and picked up the bowl of salt. He began to run back to Nicholas, but as he did, he tripped over the sheet they had pulled off of the supplies. The bowl went flying through the air, landing directly on top of Nicholas and spilling all over him. Jamie stood up abduced stared at him in horror. Wiping the salt and vinegar mixture off of him, Nicholas looked up at Jamie.

"Go!" he bellowed, beckoning at the steps. Jamie flew

down the steps and ran into the kitchen, startling Leslie and Lucinda.

"We need another salt bowl!" yelled Jamie. They looked at him, confused.

"It spilled!" he quickly explained. They moved into action. Leslie grabbed a bowl, and Jamie poured in the salt and vinegar. Lucinda grabbed a large spoon and started mixing.

"Here!" Leslie thrust the bowl at Jamie. Turning and running back up the stairs, Jamie caught a glimpse of the clock, showing they had three minutes left. Jamie climbed to the top of the staircase, where Nicholas stood, waiting. The boys began sprinkling the salt onto the wrap. Once they had emptied the bowl, there was one minute remaining. The boys stood back and watched. To their surprise, the portal began sealing itself shut, the saran wrap and salt disappearing as it closed. The boys gave each other hopeful looks. All of the sudden, a figure was coming towards them from inside the circle. It was getting closer and closer, but the portal was only halfway sealed.

"Oh no!" exclaimed Jamie, putting his hands on his head. The figure grew closer and closer, until it was almost to the entrance. Faint laughter came from it, the same laugh both Jamie and Nicholas had heard before.

"I don't think it's gonna close fast enough!" Nicholas yelled in horror. The figure was close enough now they could almost see it clearly. It was tall and slender, with a dull shade of black covering its body. Its eyes were yellow, and it had a big, creepy smile that gave Jamie chills.
"C'mon, c'mon." Nicholas muttered to himself. The portal

was almost completely closed, but now, to their horror, the Jinn began to climb through the small bit left unmended. Its long, bony fingers wrapping around the edge, slowly pulling itself through. Jamie covered his eyes, not wanting to watch its stick-like figures emerge from the circle. He heard a scream, and then everything went silent. Jamie slowly looked up, first looking at Nicholas, who still had his eyes covered. Jamie gasped when he saw what had happened. The portal had closed before the Jinn was all the way through, pushing it back into the circle. Jamie walked over to the portal. It was completely sealed. Jamie smiled and turned to Nicholas. "Nicholas! Look! It's closed! Their gone!" Jamie ran over to Nicholas, who was now uncovering his eyes. He looked as shocked as Jamie.

"They're- they're, gone?" he questioned, looking from Jamie to the portal.

"Yeah!" exclaimed Jamie, laughing. Nicholas joined in, until both boys were jumping around and yelling. Suddenly, Leslie and Lucinda appeared. They rounded the corner of the stairs and stood looking at the boys.

"They're gone!" roared Jamie.

"Really?" questioned Leslie in disbelief.

"Yes!" Jamie exclaimed. All three kids jumped around the attic, celebrating their victory. Lucinda smiled and walked over to them. They all stopped and turned to her to listen.

"You boys did very well. Now they Jinn's are trapped, but not destroyed. We must continue onto the next step tomorrow. But for tonight you guys did very well."

Lucinda nodded in approvement at the boys.

"Yeah, even if Jamie threw vinegar salt on me." Nicholas pointed to his vinegar covered self. They all laughed.

"Hey, it wasn't my fault you left the sheet on the floor." Jamie playfully argued back. Leslie rolled her eyes.

"Well the only thing that matters now is that you guys trapped the Jinn's, and that we need to do step two starting tomorrow." Leslie stated. They all nodded in agreement.

They headed to the front door, where Lucinda dismissed them.

"I'll see you guys tomorrow," she called after them. "Get some good rest!" Lucinda waved to them. They all waved back, still celebrating their achievement.

"You did great, Jamie!" Nicholas said supportively.

"Yeah," Jamie replied, rolling his eyes. "I just stood in the middle of the street like a dummy. You should've seen me. I was literally walking up and down the street, like, ten times. Then, I randomly ran into the creepy lady's house at the end of the street. These people probably think I'm crazy." Jamie gestured to the houses around them. They all howled with laughter.

"Well, I'll see you guys later," Leslie said once they had reached her house. "Bye!" Leslie ran up the the door, then disappeared inside her house, leaving Jamie and Nicholas alone. They continued walking until they had reached Nicholas's house.

"Well, tonight was crazy. But we did it right. Now we have to do it right again tomorrow." Nicholas started up the sidewalk towards his house. He turned back around. "Are you going home?" he asked.

"I think I'm going to go to the hospital to check on my mom. I know we have to finish step two for everything to go back to normal, but I wanna see if she's any better." Jamie explained.

"Cool. I hope she is. Goodnight, Jamie." Nicholas said.

"Goodnight, Nicholas."

He watched until Nicholas closed the door, then made his way towards the hospital.

He walked down the hallway to his mom's room, and knocked on the door. "Come in." he heard his dad's voice say from the other side of the door. Jamie opened the door, spotting his dad sitting on the edge of his mother's bed, holding her hand. Jamie slowly approached them, and stopped abruptly in front of his dad.

"How is she?" he questioned nervously, his sleeping mom lying peacefully on the bed. His dad smiled.

"She's doing a lot better," he answered, excitement rising in his voice. "She was looking around earlier, and she even said a couple of words. The doctors' said that she should be in full recovery soon."

Jamie grinned. "That's great." he answered, trying his best to hid the tensity in his voice. He knew if they messed up tomorrow, everyone's life was on the line. "I'm really tired.

I'm going to go ahead and get to sleep." Jamie walked over to the wooden ledge that only had a small blanket covering it. He laid down, and was soon asleep. The noises of the hospital slowly faded out, as he drifted off into sleep.

CHAPTER 11

The next morning came, and Jamie was more nervous than ever. If anything at all messed up, they would all be in danger of being taken by the Jinn's. He quickly got ready, then walked over to his mom's bed. She was doing much better, she even told Jamie goodbye and hugged him.

It was now twelve o'clock, and Jamie headed towards Leslie's house where they were all supposed to be meeting. As Jamie approached her house, he saw her and Nicholas standing in the front yard talking. "Hey guys." he greeted them.

"Hey Jamie." they replied at the same time.

"Are you all ready?" Jamie questioned.

"I guess we have to be." Nicholas said.

"Leslie, do you have the binder?" Jamie asked.

Leslie nodded and pulled out the thick binder with a lot of unnecessary pages added to it. She flipped it open, and began reading.

"We must carefully enter the portal, with a taser and food."

"Why do we need that?" interrupted Nicholas, raising his eyebrows.

"I don't know," Leslie remarked annoyedly. "That's just what it says. Then it says we need to distract the Jinn's with the food," Leslie emphasized this sentence dramatically, staring at Nicholas.

He shrugged. "Who knew you could distract Jinn's with food."

Leslie rolled her eyes. "Then while they're distracted we rescue the people taken into the circle, and bring them back to our side. After that, we must go back into the circle and destroy the master. If all goes as planned, after we finish that everything should be normal again." Leslie slammed the binder shut and looked at the boys.

 "Where are we going to get a taser?" questioned Nicholas.

"Follow me." Jamie replied.

 Jamie led the group up the street and to the police station. "So we're gonna steal a taser?" Nicholas asked, shocked.

"Have any other ideas, genius?" Jamie snapped back.

They casually entered the office, smiling at the officer behind the front desk. He smiled back, then looked back down at his laptop.

"C'mon." whispered Jamie. The group sneaked into John's office, without anyone noticing. "There has to be a taser in here somewhere." Jamie said, rummaging through the drawers. A few moments later, Jamie spotted what appeared to be a taser at the bottom of one of the drawers. "Aha!" Jamie pulled out the taser.

"Good work!" Nicholas whisper-screamed at him.

They filed back out into the office, then headed towards the door like nothing had happened. "Now what do we do?" asked Nicholas, when they were several blocks from the station.

"I guess we can go over to Lucinda's, since she didn't mention anything about it having to be dark." remarked Leslie. They all nodded in agreement.

Once they were at Lucinda's house, she led them into the kitchen.

"We need food to get the attention of the Jinn's." she explained. They gathered the most appetizing food they could find. Muffins, cupcakes, and pastries soon flooded the backpack Lucinda had brought from upstairs.

"Ok," Lucinda stated, clasping her hands together. "Now we need a taser, just in case the food plan doesn't work, but mostly for the master." Lucinda looked around at the kids. "Did any of you bring one?" Jamie held up the taser they had taken from John's office.

Lucinda grinned. "Excellent!" she exclaimed. "Now, who's ready?" Lucinda picked up the backpacks and handed them to the kids.

"Already?" Nicholas asked in alarm.

Lucinda looked at him. "This could take awhile. It would be best to start now, but if you really want to-"

"We're ready." answered Jamie confidently.

They packed the backpacks upstairs, and stood in front of the portal.

"Now, this is very dangerous. It is important you follow me and don't go off by yourself. Don't make any loud noises, and do exactly what I do." Lucinda took a deep breath, and adjusted herself so she was standing directly in the center of the portal. She raised her arms, then as if it were nothing, vanished into the circle. The group looked at each other nervously, then they too lined up in front of the portal.

"It's all or nothing." Jamie stated, studying the portal. It had a purple glow, that could mesmerize you if you stared too long.

"Here we go." Leslie said. They stepped into the purple glow, and when they stepped out, it was a whole new world. Purple and blue colors surrounded them, bits and pieces of random chunks floating in mid air. It was like a galaxy. Like somewhere that only existed in your dreams. Everything seemed to be moving in slow motion, and there was no direction whatsoever. It seemed to be the exact same in every location, everywhere they looked. It was very peaceful, and Jamie couldn't understand why such evil things lived in such a breathtaking spot.

"Wow." Nicholas remarked, scanning his surroundings.

"Come, children, follow me." Lucinda was already headed towards a rather large chunk of the block. The kids followed. As they approached the block, Jamie noticed that it wasn't just a block, but a hang out for Jinn's. There were hundreds maybe thousands sitting inside. Lucinda beckoned to the kids to follow her, and they crept around the side to where they had a better view. They seemed to be having a good time. They were laughing and playing with each other, as if they were almost as normal as people. Lucinda pulled out the backpack full of food, and prepared it to be devoured by the beasts.

"Just sit back and watch." Lucinda pulled out a handful of pastries, and threw them into the din of monsters. The beasts raced towards the food, as if it was the most sacred thing in the world. "How delicious!" one cried, shoved a whole pastry in his mouth.

"It taste like heaven!" cried another, in its deep, raspy voice. Lucinda gestured to the kids, and they all began throwing things into the block, to be devoured by the Jinn's. After they had ran out of food, Lucinda hurriedly walked away towards another block, similar to the one they had just left.

"That's where they keep everyone who they've taken so far," Lucinda explained. "They don't move them until they've taken everyone needed to make their empire." Lucinda led them inside the block, which was similar to a mansion. It looked exactly like the world outside. Purple and blue colors filled the entrance, pictures of what appeared to be previously taken victims lined the walls. Jamie shivered. Making sure the coast was clear, Lucinda continued to a hallway that had at least fifteen doors. She led them to the very last door, a dark wooden color. There was a sign on it that read, *October.* Slowly opening it, Lucinda peaked around the corner. Seeing nothing, she continued the rest of the way in. The group followed, being led down row after row of boxes. Finally, they came to a clearing in the back of the room, which looked to be like one giant bedroom. Except it wasn't. It didn't contain a bed, chair, or one piece of furniture. The only things inside were stone benches, filling most of the room. Lucinda turned around to face Jamie, Leslie, and Nicholas.

"Ok, you're friends are somewhere in here. We need to find them quickly and get out before the Jinn's find us."

Lucinda and the group searched around the room, until finally, they spotted Zach and Freddie sitting on one of the benches in the very back of the room. Jamie gasped and ran over to them, followed by the others. Zach looked as if he hadn't slept in days, dark rings circling his eyes, dirt covered his body and his black hair ruffled. Freddie looked frightened, but relieved to see Jamie and the others.

After a few minutes of conversation, Lucinda broke them up.

"We can save the celebrating for after the master is gone and everyone is back safely at home." Lucinda led them back out of the block, and towards the portal.

"Wait!" Zach exclaimed. "I want to stay and help get rid of the master. I want to destroy him." he said angrily.

"Me too!" Freddie cried. He's been nothing but

disrespectful to us and it's time for payback. Freddie looked around at the group.

Lucinda nodded. "Very well then. Let's go!"

After about ten minutes of walking around the large galaxy, they finally spotted a huge block, at least three times the size as the others.

"I'm guessing that's where the master lives." Nicholas observed.

"You guessed right." Lucinda responded.

They made their way closer to the castle, stopping abruptly when they heard a voice behind them.

"Well, well, well," a deep, raspy voice from behind them called. "What do we have here?"

A large, bulkier version of the Jinn's stood behind them. He stood at least eight feet tall, and had razor sharp teeth that could bite through rock. The groups eyes widened. Jamie quickly pulled out the taser and pointed it towards the monster. The master stared at Jamie for a second, and then let out a deep, bellowing laugh.

"Silly boy, you think that's going to stop me? I've been through worse." The beast smiled mockingly at Jamie.

"You took my friends and family, and now you're trying to destroy our world, to take all of us here, in this place, for what? There's nothing valuable here. There's no reason for you to have us. There's no reason you should have us. And that's why we're here. To prevent that from happening."

Without thinking, Jamie held down the button on the taser, and shocked the monster. It shook for a while, then laughed again.

"You think you humans are so smart, always thinking your inventions are enough to kill a monster like me." The monster's eyes narrowed. "And now you'll see that there isn't always a happy ending." The monster stretched out his arms, then began to come at them.

"Run!" Jamie roared.

They took off towards the castle, the master close behind. It's fingernails ripping into the earth as it tore across the land, quickly gaining on them.

"In here!" Zach slid around the corner into a small room, just big enough for the six of them to fit. Everything went silent.

"Is it gone?" whispered Nicholas.

All of the sudden, the beast ripped through the door as if it were sand, and grabbed Freddie. "No!" exclaimed Jamie. But it was too late. The monster ripped Freddie to shreds, then began to come for them. Shielding his eyes, Jamie listened as the monster grew closer and closer. He could now feel his breath on his neck. It trickled down his neck, chilling his spine. The beast was now enclosing on Jamie, it's bony fingers slowly gripping onto Jamie's arms.

Just as the monster began to pick him up, it suddenly froze, let out a yelp, and threw Jamie onto the ground, where he landed hard on top of a piece of wood. He groaned, looking up to see what had stopped the monster. To his surprise, he saw that the wall was pouring out a foul smelling black liquid, which had now completely covered the beast, and when it receded, there was nothing left. Not even the master. They all stared for a moment longer, not believing what had just happened.

"The wall just killed the master." Nicholas said in disbelief. They all looked around, then not saying a word, exited the castle. As they headed towards the portal, they were all filled with sorrow, disbelief, and excitement all at the same time. The monster may have gotten Freddie, but the wall had saved them by trapping the master, and now they were responsible for saving the world and conquering the Jinn's.

"We just defeated them!" Jamie exclaimed, still in shock. "Now everything's going to be normal again!"

The group celebrated all the way back to the portal, where they watched the life inside the circle slowly be sucked away, until there was nothing left. The portal began to disappear, and before long, it was completely gone, with no evidence it ever existed.

"I can't believe we really did that!" Jamie exclaimed, as they all celebrated with hot chocolate down in Lucinda's kitchen.

"Yeah. Thank you guys for saving my life," Zach started. "Not that you didn't have a little help from that wall." They all laughed.

"Yes, you all did well. I have to say I am a little shocked." Lucinda chimed in.

"We couldn't have done it without you." Leslie told Lucinda.

She smiled. "We certainly made a great team." Lucinda responded.

After celebrating their victory, Jamie went to the hospital to see his mom. He entered the room, his mom smiling at him when she saw him.

"Jamie!" she exclaimed. She held out her arms for Jamie to give her a hug. He smiled and ran over to her.

"I missed you." he sobbed into her gown.

She stroked his head. "Don't cry. The doctors' said I made a great recovery and could go home tomorrow." She let go of him. "I'll take off work for awhile so we can spend some time together, how about that?" she smiled.

Jamie grinned and nodded. "That would be great."

As he went to sleep that night, all he could think about is how they had won. No one but Lucinda and his friends knew about it, not even his parents. But that was okay. He knew he saved the world and that was all that mattered.

CHAPTER 12

Jamie and his friends had indeed turned the world back to normal. He went back to school with his friends, where they all had to make up crazy stories about what had happened with Zach, which turned out to make them pretty popular. At lunch, random kids he didn't even know would ask about Zach. Even Jack and Henry were treating them nice, which was fine by Jamie. News had spread all around the world about Zach. He was on the news, which made him basically a celebrity. Everywhere he went, he got questions about his experiences of 'coming back to life'. Lucinda and the group were still the only people who actually knew what happened, and they knew Zach never came back to life, because he had never died in the first place. The news even spread to Zach's dad, and he traveled all the way to Connecticut from Ohio to see Zach. The file turned out to be wrong, and he had never moved back to Connecticut. He actually turned out to be a pretty good person. Zach seemed happy to be able to see him again. Rosa had even showed up to Freddie's funeral and brought flowers.

Zach was back on the baseball team, and was treated like some kind of hero by all of his teammates. The coach now favored him and let him play in every game. So far, they were undefeated and Zach had hit two more home runs since the last time he played before everything happened.

They all still visited Lucinda, and she was glad to have their company. She told them stories about different worlds, and about some of the books that she owned. They were all about paranormal things, or different dimensions, Some were even instructional books about how to defeat the things that lived in the different worlds. Nicholas had even began to like the cats. She wasn't a witch at all, like they had first thought. She may be a little strange, but she had now become one of their closest friends.

Jamie's parents had taken off weekends so they could spend time with him. His mom was much better, and Jamie's relationship with his parents was now fixed. They usually went on picnics or on a walk, or sometimes they just sat at the table and talked.

Now that the world was back to normal, Jamie had again started working on his robots.

"Ok, Tommy, here we go." Jamie switched on the robot, his buttons flashing, indicating he was now alive. Jamie waved his hand in front of him, and in response, Tommy waved back.

"Yes!" exclaimed Jamie. The robot had finally learned to respond. As Jamie was celebrating his success, he heard a knock on his door.

"Jamie, your friends are here." he heard his mom call through the door.

"Ok." he answered back. He turned off Tommy, and ran downstairs to meet his friends.

"Hey Jamie." greeted Leslie.

"Wanna come to Lucinda's with us?" questioned Nicholas.

"Definitely." responded Jamie.

As they walked to Lucinda's, Jamie couldn't help but think about Freddie, and how the world was actually normal again. They didn't have to worry about Jinn's anymore, and they were all finally having a good time. Even though everything was normal again, he was still sad he couldn't save Freddie. *I wonder what it would be like if he was here now*, wondered Jamie. *He never even knew about Lucinda, or what had happened to him. He was clueless.*

Snapping out of his thoughts, Jamie saw Leslie and Nicholas running down the street laughing. Jamie smiled, then ran to catch up with them. Things in his life were finally good, he just hoped they stayed this way.

—

—

ABOUT THE AUTHOR

Lauren Mitchell is a middle school student in Owensboro, Kentucky. She enjoys writing, playing the violin and ukulele, and playing with her three cats, Sophie, Jonas, and Jingles.

www.ingramcontent.com/pod-product-compliance
Lightning Source LLC
Chambersburg PA
CBHW022106050726
47591CB00002B/687